MW01281840

Places of My Infancy

A Memory

•

GIUSEPPE TOMASI DI LAMPEDUSA

Translated by Archibald Colquhoun

A NEW DIRECTIONS PEARL

Copyright © 1961 by Giangiacomo Feltrinelli Editore
Translation copyright © 1995 by Archibald Colquhoun
Copyright © 2012 by New Directions

All rights reserved. Except for brief passages quoted in a newspaper, magazine, ra-
dio, television, or website review, no part of this book may be reproduced in any
form or by any means, electronic or mechanical, including photocopying and re-
cording, or by any information storage and retrieval system, without permission
in writing from the Publisher.

Manufactured in the United States of America
New Directions Books are printed on acid-free paper
First published as a Pearl (NDP1241) by New Directions in 2012
Design by Erik Rieselbach

Library of Congress Cataloging-in-Publication Data
Tomasi di Lampedusa, Giuseppe, 1896–1957.
[Racconti. English]
Places of my infancy / Giuseppe Tomasi di Lampedusa ; translated
by Archibald Colquhoun.
p. cm.
"A New Directions Pearl."
Includes bibliographical references and index.
ISBN 978-0-8112-2038-5 (acid free paper)
1. Tomasi di Lampedusa, Giuseppe, 1896–1957—Family. 2. Authors, Italian—
20th century—Biography. 3. Sicily (Italy)—Biography. I. Colquhoun,
Archibald. II. Title.
PQ4843.O53R3313 2012
853'.914—dc23

10 9 8 7 6 5 4 3

New Directions Books are published for James Laughlin
by New Directions Publishing Corporation
80 Eighth Avenue, New York 10011

PLACES OF MY INFANCY

WITH EVERYONE, I THINK, memories of early childhood consist of a series of visual impressions, many very clear but lacking any sense of chronology. To write a "chronicle" of one's own childhood is, it seems, impossible; however honest one might set out to be one would eventually give a false impression, often with glaring anachronisms. I shall therefore adopt the method of grouping my subjects together, so trying to give an overall impression in space rather than by sequence of time. I will touch on the background of my childhood and of the people forming part of it; also of my feelings, though I will not try to follow the development of these from their origins.

I can promise to say nothing that is untrue, but I shall not want to say *all*; and I reserve the right to lie by omission. Unless I change my mind.

One of the oldest memories I can set exactly in time, as it is connected with a fact verifiable historically, goes back to the 30th of July 1900, and so to the time when I was a few days over three and a half years old.

I was with my mother in her dressing room, with her maid (probably Teresa from Turin). It was a rectangular room whose windows gave on to a pair of balconies projecting from the shorter sides, one of them looking over a narrow garden that separated our house from the Oratory of S. Zita, the other over a small inner courtyard. The dressing-table, kidney-shaped, with a pink material showing through its glass top and legs enwrapped in a kind of white lace petticoat, was set facing the balcony overlooking the little garden; on it, as well as brushes and toilet implements, stood a big mirror in a frame also made of mirror, decorated with stars and other glass ornaments which were a delight to me.

It was about eleven in the morning, I think, and I can see the great light of summer coming through the open French windows, whose shutters were closed.

My mother was combing her hair with the help of her maid, and I do not know what I could have been doing, sitting on the floor in the middle of the room. I don't know if my nurse, Elvira the Sienese, was with us too, but I think not.

Suddenly we hear hurried steps coming up the little inner staircase communicating with my father's apartments on the lower or *mezzanine* floor directly beneath; he enters without knocking, and utters some phrase in an excited tone. I remember his manner very well, but not his words nor their sense.

I can "see" still, though, the effect they produced; my mother dropped the long-handled silver brush she was holding, Teresa said, "*Bon Signour!*" and the whole room was in consternation.

My father had come to announce the assassination of King Umberto at Monza the evening before, the 29th of July 1900. I repeat that I "see" every streak of light and shade from the balcony, "hear" my father's excited voice, the sound of the brush falling on the glass tabletop, good Teresa's exclamation in Piedmontese, that I "feel" the sense of dismay which overwhelmed us; but all this remains personal, detached from the news of the King's death. The historic meaning, as it were, was told me later, and may serve to explain the persistence of the scene in my memory.

Another of the memories which I can clearly distinguish is that of the Messina earthquake (28th December 1908). The shock was certainly felt at Palermo, but I have no memory of that; I suppose it did not interrupt my sleep. But I can see distinctly the hands of my grandfather's big English pendulum-clock, which was then incongruously located in the big winter drawing room, stopped at the fatal hour of twenty past five; and I can still hear one of my uncles (I think Ferdinando who was mad about watchmaking) explain to me that it had been stopped by an earthquake during the night. Then I remember that same evening, about half past seven, being in my grandparents' dining room (I used often to be present at their dinner as it took place before mine) when an uncle, probably the same Ferdinando, came in with an evening paper which announced "serious damage and numerous victims at Messina from this morning's earthquake."

I speak of "my grandparents' dining room," but I should say my grandmother's, because my grandfather had been dead a year and a month.

This memory is much less lively visually than the first, though much more exact on the other hand from the point of view of a "thing that happened."

Some days later there arrived from Messina my cousin Filippo who had lost his father and mother in the earthquake. He went to stay with my cousins the Piccolos, together with his cousin Adamo, and I remember going there to pay him a visit on a bleak rainy winter's day. I remember that he had a camera (already!) which he had taken care to keep with him as he escaped from the ruins of his house in Via della Rovere, and how on a table by a window he drew the outlines of warships and discussed with Casimiro the caliber of the guns and the emplacement of the turrets; his insouciant attitude amid the dreadful misadventures he had undergone was criticized at the time by his family, though it was charitably ascribed to shock resulting from the disaster— this was said to be prevalent among all the survivors of Messina. It was later more accurately put down to a cold nature which only caught fire in addressing technical questions such as, precisely, photography and the turrets on the early dreadnoughts.

I can still see my mother's grief when, quite a few days later, came news of her sister Lina's and her brother-in-law's bodies having been found. I can see my mother, dressed in a short cape of moiré Astrakhan, sobbing in a big armchair in the green drawing room, an armchair in which no one ever sat, though it's the very one in which I "see" my great-grandmother sitting. Big army wagons were going round the streets collecting clothes and blankets for refugees; one passed along Via di Lampedusa and I handed woollen blankets from one of our balconies over to a soldier standing up on a cart and almost level with the balcony. This soldier was an artilleryman, with orange braid on his blue forage cap; I can still see his rubicund face and hear his "Thank you, m'boy," in a mainland accent. I have a memory, too, of a rumor going round that the refugees, who were lodged everywhere, even in boxes at theaters, were behaving "most indecently" among themselves, and of my father saying with a smile, "They feel an urge to replace the dead," an allusion which I understood perfectly.

I retain no clear recollection of my Aunt Lina, who died in the earthquake; (her demise opened the sequence of tragic deaths among my mother's sisters, which provides a sampling of the three kinds of death by violence—accident, murder and suicide). She seldom came to Palermo: I do remember her husband, though, with his lively pair of eyes behind his glasses, and an unkempt, grizzled little beard.

There is another day also clearly stamped on my memory; I cannot get the date exactly, but it was certainly a long time before the Messina earthquake and shortly after King

Umberto's death, I think. We were guests of the Florios at their villa of Favignana, at the height of summer. I remember Erica, my nurse, coming to wake me up earlier than usual, about seven, hurriedly passing a sponge full of cold water over my face and then dressing me with great care. I was dragged downstairs, went out through a little side-door to the garden, then made to climb up on to the villa's main entrance veranda overlooking the sea, and reached by a flight of some six or seven steps. I remember the blinding sun of that early morning of July or August. On the veranda, which was protected from the sun by great curtains of orange cloth swelling and flapping like sails in the sea breeze (I can still hear the sound), my mother, Signora Florio (the "divinely lovely" Franca) and others were sitting on cane-chairs. In the center of the group sat a very old, very bent lady with an aquiline nose, enwrapped in widow's weeds which were waving wildly about in the wind. I was brought before her; she said a few words which I did not understand and, bending down even farther, gave me a kiss on the forehead. (I must have been very small indeed if a lady sitting down had to bend down even farther to kiss me.) After this I was taken back to my room, stripped of my finery, redressed in more modest garments and led on to the beach to join the Florio children and others: with them I bathed and we stayed for a long time under a broiling sun playing our favorite game, which was searching in the sand for pieces of deep red coral occasionally to be found there.

That afternoon it was revealed that the old lady had been Eugénie, ex-Empress of the French, whose yacht was anchored off Favignana; she had dined with the Florios the night before (without of course my knowing anything about it) and had paid a farewell visit at seven next morning, (thus with imperial nonchalance inflicting real torture on my mother and on Signora Florio), in the course of which her hosts had wished to present to her the younger members of the household. It appears that the words she uttered before kissing me were: "*Quel joli petit!*"

During these last few days (mid-June, 1955) I have been rereading Stendhal's *Henri Brulard*. I had not read it since long ago in 1922, when I must have still been obsessed by "explicit beauty" and "subjective interest," for I remember not liking the book.

Now I cannot but agree with anyone who judges it to be Stendhal's masterpiece; it has an immediacy of feeling, an obvious sincerity, a remarkable attempt to sweep away accumulated memories and reach the essence. And what lucidity of style! What a mass of reflections, the more precious for being common to all men!

I should like to try and do the same. Indeed it seems obligatory. When one reaches the decline of life it is imperative to try and gather together as many as possible of the sensations which have passed through our particular organism. Few can succeed in thus creating a masterpiece (Rousseau, Stendhal, Proust) but all should find it possible to preserve in some such way things which without this slight effort would be lost forever. To keep a diary, or write down one's own memories at a certain age, should be a duty "State-imposed"; material thus accumulated would have inestimable value after three or four generations; many of the psychological and historical problems that assail humanity would be resolved. There are no memoirs, even those written by insignificant people, which do not include social and graphic details of first-rate importance.

The extraordinary interest that Defoe's novels aroused is due to the fact that they are near-diaries, brilliant though apocryphal. What, one wonders, would genuine ones have been like? Imagine, say, the diary of a Parisian procuress of the *Régence*, or the memories of Byron's valet during the Venetian period!

I shall try to follow the *Henri Brulard* method as closely as possible, even in describing the "seedlings" of the principal scenes.

But I find I cannot follow Stendhal in "quality" of memory. He interprets his childhood as a time when he was bullied and tyrannized. For me childhood is a lost paradise. Everyone was good to me—I was king of the home—even people later hostile to me were then "*aux petits soins.*"

So the reader (who won't exist) must expect to be led meandering through a lost Earthly Paradise. If it bores him, I don't mind.

II

Casa Lampedusa

FIRST OF ALL, our home. I loved it with utter abandon, and still love it now when for the last twelve years it has been no more than a memory. Until a few months before its destruction I used to sleep in the room where I was born, five yards away from the spot where my mother's bed had stood when she gave me birth. And in that house, in that very room maybe, I was glad to feel a certainty of dying. All my other homes (very few, actually, apart from hotels) have merely been roofs which have served to shelter me from rain and sun, not homes in the traditional and venerable sense of that word. And especially the one I have now, which I don't like at all, which I bought to please my wife and which I'm delighted to have bequeathed to her, because the fact is it's not my house.

So it will be very painful for me to evoke my dead Beloved as she was until 1929 in her integrity and beauty, and as she continued after all to be until 5th April 1943, the day on which bombs brought from beyond the Atlantic searched her out and destroyed her.

The first impression that remains with me is that of her vastness, and this impression owes nothing to the magnifying process which affects all that surrounds one's childhood, but to actual reality. When I saw the area covered by the unsightly ruins I found they were about 1600 square yards in extent. With only ourselves living in one wing, my paternal grandparents in another, my bachelor uncles on the second floor, for twenty years it was all at my disposal, with its three courtyards, four terraces, garden, huge staircases, halls, corridors, stables, little rooms on the *mezzanine* for servants and offices—a real kingdom for a boy alone, a kingdom either empty or sparsely populated by figures unanimously well-disposed.

At no point on earth, I'm sure, has sky ever stretched more violently blue than it did above our enclosed terrace, never has sun thrown gentler rays than those penetrating the half-closed shutters of the "green drawing room," never have damp-marks on a courtyard's outer walls presented shapes more stimulating to the imagination than those at my home.

I loved everything about it: the irregularity of its walls, the number of its drawing rooms, the stucco of its ceilings, the nasty smell from my grandparents' kitchen, the scent of violets in my mother's dressing room, the stuffiness of its stables, the good feel of polished leather in its tack rooms, the mystery of some unfinished apartments on the top floor, the huge coach house in which our carriages were kept; a whole world full of sweet mysteries, of surprises ever renewed and ever fresh.

I was its absolute master and would run continually through its vast expanses, climbing the great staircase from the courtyard to the loggia on the roof, from which could be seen the sea and Mount Pellegrino and the whole city as far as Porta Nuova and Monreale. And knowing how by devious routes and turns to avoid inhabited rooms, I would feel alone and dictatorial, followed often only by my friend Tom running excitedly at my heels, with his red tongue dangling from his dear black snout.

The house (and I prefer to call it a house rather than a palace, a word which has been debased in Italy, applied as it is nowadays even to blocks fifteen stories high), was tucked away in one of the most secluded streets of old Palermo, in Via di Lampedusa, at number 17, the uneven number's evil omen then serving only to add a pleasantly sinister flavor to the joy that it dispensed. (When later the stables were transformed into storerooms we asked for the number to be changed, and it became 23 when the end was near; so number 17 had after all been lucky.)

The street was secluded but not so very narrow, and well paved; nor was it dirty as might be thought, for opposite our entrance and along the whole length of the building extended the old Pietrapersia palace which had no shops or dwellings on the ground floor, its austere, clean front in local white and yellow punctuated by numerous windows protected by enormous grilles, conferring on it the dignified and gloomy air of an old convent or state prison. The bomb explosions later flung many of those heavy grilles into our rooms opposite, with what happy effect on the old stucco work and Murano chandeliers can be imagined.

But if Via di Lampedusa was decent enough, for the whole length of our house at least, the streets into it were not; Via Bara all'Olivella, leading into Piazza Massimo, was crawling with poverty and squalid cellars, and depressing to pass along. It became slightly better when Via Roma was cut through, but there always remained a good stretch of filth and horrors to traverse.

The façade of the house had no particular architectural merit: it was white with wide borders round windows of sulphur yellow, in purest Sicilian style of the seventeenth and eighteenth centuries in fact. It extended along Via di Lampedusa for some seventy yards or so, and had nine big balconies on the front. There were two gateways almost at the corners of the building, of enormous width as they used to be made in olden days to allow carriages to turn in from narrow streets. And in fact there was easy room even for the four-horsed teams which my father drove with mastery to race meetings at La Favorita.

Just inside the main gate which we always used, the first on the left as one faces the façade, almost at the corner of Via Bara, and separated from the corner of the building by no more than a couple of yards' frontage on to which opened the grilled window of the porter's lodge, one entered a short paved gateway, its two side walls of white stucco supported by a low step. On the left was the porter's nook (which led through to his living quarters), with the fine mahogany door in the middle of which there was a big opaque glass pane with our coat of arms. And immediately after, still on the left preceding the two steps and the entrance to the "grand staircase," with its double-leaved doors also in mahogany and glass (clear this time and devoid of any coat of arms), right in front of the right-hand stairway there was a colonnade of fine gray Billiemi stone that supported the overhanging *tocchetto* or gallery. Beyond this gate in fact lay the main courtyard, cobbled and divided into sections by rows of flagstones. At the far end three great arches, also supported on columns of Billiemi stone, bore a terrace which linked the two wings of the house at that point.

Beneath the first colonnade, to the right of the entrance gates there were several plants, mostly palms, in wooden tubs varnished green, and at the end there was a plaster statue of some Greek god or other, standing. Also at the end, and parallel to the entrance, there was the door to the tack room.

The main staircase was a very fine one, all in gray Billiemi, with two flights of fifteen steps or so each, set between yellowish walls. Where the second flight began there was a wide oblong landing with two mahogany doors, one facing each flight of stairs; the one giving on to the first flight led to the quarters of the mezzanine devoted to the Administration and called "the Accounts Office," the other to a minute cubbyhole wherein the footmen used to change their livery.

These two doors were decorated with a cornice also in Billiemi of Empire style, and they were surmounted at the height of the first floor each one with bulging little gilt balconies, which both opened on to the little entrance hall to our grandparents' apartments.

I forgot to say that just past the entrance to the stairs, but on the exterior, in the courtyard, hung the red cord of a bell which the porter was supposed to ring in order to warn servants of their mistress's return, or the approach of visitors. The number of rings, which the porters gave with great skill, obtaining, I don't know how, sharp separate strokes without any tiresome tinkling, was rigorously laid down by protocol; four strokes for my grandmother the princess and two for her visitors, three for my mother the duchess and one for her visitors. But misunderstandings would occur, so that when at times my mother, grandmother, and some friend picked up on the way entered in the same carriage, a real concert would ring out of four plus three plus two strokes which were never ending. The masters, my grandfather and father, left and returned without any bell ringing for them at all.

The second flight of stairs came out on to the wide luminous *tocchetto*, which was a gallery with the spaces between its columns filled in, for reasons of comfort, by big windows with opaque lozenge-shaped panes. This contained a few sparse pieces of furniture, some big portraits of ancestors, and a large table to the left on which were put letters on arrival (it was then I read a postcard addressed to my uncle Ciccio from Paris, on which some French tart had written: "*Dis à Moffo qu'il est un mufle*"), two pretty chests and a plaster statue of Pandora on the point of opening the fatal box, surrounded by plants. At the end, facing the head of the stairs, there was a door, always closed, which gave directly on to the "green drawing room" (a door which much later was to become the entrance to our quarters), and to the right of the stairs, the entrance to the "great hall," guarded by an ever-open door, in embroidered red brocade, the upper part displaying our coat of arms and that of the Valdina in color in the glass.

The "great hall" was immense, flagged in white and gray marble, with three balconies over Via di Lampedusa and one over the Lampedusa courtyard, a dead-end extension of Via Bara. It was divided by an arch which split it in two unequal parts, the first smaller and the second vastly bigger. To my parents' great regret, its decoration was entirely modern, as in 1848 a shell had destroyed the fine painted ceiling and irreparably damaged the wall frescoes. For a long time, it seems, a fig tree flourished there. The hall was done up when my grandfather married, that is in 1866 or '67, all in white stucco with a wainscot of gray marble. In the center of the ceiling of each of the two parts a coat of arms was depicted; opposite the entrance there was a big walnut table on which visitors left their hats and

capes; then there were a few chests and the odd chair. It
was in this great hall that the footmen waited, lounging in
their chairs and ready to hurry out into the *tocchetto* at the
sound of that bell below.

After coming in by the door in red brocade which I've
mentioned, if one turned towards the left-hand wall, one
found another door similarly covered but in green, which
gave access to our apartment; if one turned left one had to
go on through until on the right one reached a little staircase and a door leading to my grandparents' quarters, beginning actually with the "little room" with the two little
balconies which overlooked the stairs.

A door with green hangings gave on to the antechamber, with six portraits of ancestors hung above its balcony
entrance and its two doors, walls of gray silk, and the odd
piece of dark furniture. And from there the eye fell on a
perspective of drawing rooms extending one after the
other for the length of the façade, Here for me began the
magic of light, which in a city with so intense a sun as
Palermo is concentrated or variegated according to the
weather, even in narrow streets. This light was sometimes
diluted by the silk curtains hanging before balconies, or
heightened by beating on some gilt frame or yellow damask chair which reflected it back; sometimes, particularly in summer, these rooms were dark, yet through the
closed blinds filtered a sense of the luminous power that
was outside; or sometimes at certain hours a single ray
would penetrate straight and clear as that of Sinai, popu-

lated with myriads of dust particles and going to vilify the colors of carpets, uniformly ruby-red throughout all the drawing rooms: a real sorcery of illumination and color which entranced my mind forever. Sometimes I rediscover this luminous quality in some old palace or church, and it would wrench at my heart were I not ready to brush it aside with some "wicked joke."[1]

After the antechamber came the "*lambris*" room, so called because its walls were covered halfway up by paneling of inlaid walnut; next the so-called "supper" room, its walls covered with dark flowered orange-colored silk, part of which still survives as wall-coverings in my wife's room now. And there was the great ballroom with its enameled floor and its ceiling on which delicious gold and yellow twirls framed mythological scenes where with rude energy and amid swirling robes crowded all the deities of Olympus.

After that came my mother's boudoir, very lovely, its ceiling scattered with flowers and branches of old colored stucco, in a design gentle and corporeal as a piece of music by Mozart.

And after that one entered my mother's bedroom, which was very big; the principal wall where[2] there was the room at the corner of the house with a balcony (the last one) on Via Lampedusa, and one on the garden of the oratory of Santa Zita. The decorations in wood, stucco

1 In English in the Italian text. (Trs.)
2 The Italian text here appears to be corrupted. (Trs.)

and paint in this room were among the finest in the house.

From the drawing room known as the "*lambris*" room, going left one entered the "green drawing room," which led into the "yellow drawing room" and hence into a room which started out as my day-nursery, later to be turned into a little red drawing room, the room which we most frequented, and which later became a library. This place had on the left (entering from the yellow drawing room) a window on to the great courtyard and in the same wall a glass-paneled door giving on to the terrace. At right angles with these openings there was first a door (later bricked up) which led into a little room which used to be my grandfather's bathroom (it even had a marble bath-tub) and which served as repository for my toys, and another glass-paneled door giving on to the small terrace.

III

The Journey

BUT THE HOUSE in Palermo had dependencies in the country which multiplied its charms. These were four: Santa Margherita Belice, a villa at Bagherìa, a palace at Torretta, and a country house at Raitano. Then there was also the old home of the family at Palma and the castle of Montechiaro, but to those we never went.

The favorite was Santa Margherita, in which we would spend long months even of winter. It was one of the loveliest country houses I have ever seen. Built in 1680, it had been completely restored about 1810 by Prince Cutò on the occasion of a long sojourn there made by Ferdinand IV and Maria Carolina, forced to reside in Sicily during the years Murat was reigning in Naples. Afterwards, though, it had not been abandoned as were all other houses in Sicily, but constantly looked after, restored and enriched until the days of my grandmother Cutò, who, having lived in France until the age of twenty, had not inherited the Sicilian aversion for country life; she was in residence there almost continuously and brought it "up-to-date" (for the Second Empire, of course, which was not very different from the general standard of comfort throughout Europe until 1914).

The charm of adventure, of the not wholly comprehensible, which is so much part of my memories of Santa Margherita, began with the journey there. This was an enterprise full of discomforts and delights. At that time there were no automobiles; around 1905 the only one that circulated around Palermo was old Signora Giovanna Florio's "électrique." A train left the Lolli railway station at ten past five in the morning. So we had to get up at half past three. Awakening at that hour was always nasty and made all the more miserable for me by the fact that it was the time at which I was given castor oil when I had stomachache. Servants and cooks had already left the day before. We were bundled into two closed landaus: in the first my father and mother, the governess Anna I, let's say, and myself; in the second Teresa, or Concettina maybe, my mother's maid, Ferrara, our accountant, a native of Santa Margherita and coming to spend the holidays with his family, and Paolo, my father's valet. Another vehicle followed I think, with luggage and hampers for luncheon.

It was usually about the end of June and dawn would be just spreading over the deserted streets. Across Piazza Politeama and Via Dante (then called Via Esposizione) we reached the Lolli railway station, where we packed into the train for Trapani. Trains then had no corridors, and so no lavatories; and when I was very small there was brought along for my use a chamber pot in ghastly brown china bought on purpose and flung out of the window before reaching our destination. The ticket collector would do his rounds by grappling along the exterior of the carriages, and all at once we would see his braided cap and black-gloved hand rising outside.

For hours then we crossed the lovely, desperately sad landscape of western Sicily; it must have been I think just exactly the same as Garibaldi's Thousand had found it on landing—Carini, Cinisi, Zucco, Partinico; then the line went along the sea, the rails seeming laid on the sand itself; the sun, already hot, was broiling us in our iron box. Thermos flasks did not exist, and there were no refreshments to be expected at any station. The train next cut inland, among stony hills and fields of mown corn, yellow as the manes of lions. Eventually at eleven we reached Castelvetrano, then far from being the spry, thrusting little town it is now; it was a dreary place, with open drains and pigs walking in the main street; and flies by the billion. At the station, which had already been roasting under the sun for six hours, were waiting our carriages, two landaus fitted with yellow curtains.

At half past eleven we set off again; for an hour as far as Partanna the road was level and easy, across fine, cultivated country; we began to recognize places we knew, a pair of majolica negroes' heads on the entrance pillars of a villa, an iron cross commemorating a murder;

as we drew closer beneath Partanna, however, the scene changed: three Carabinieri appeared, a sergeant and two troopers on horseback, the napes of their necks protected by patches of white stuff like horsemen in Fattori's pictures, who were to accompany us all the way to Santa Margherita. The road became mountainous: around us unrolled the immeasurable scenery of feudal Sicily, desolate, breathless, oppressed by a leaden sun. We looked about for a tree under whose shade to lunch; but there were only scraggy olives which gave no shelter from the sun. Eventually an abandoned peasant's hut was found, half in ruins, but its windows carefully closed. In its shade we alighted and ate; succulent things mostly. Slightly apart, the Carabinieri, who had bread, meat, cakes and bottles sent over to them, made a gay luncheon of their own, untroubled by the burning sun. At the end of the meal the sergeant would come up holding a brimming glass: "I thank Your Excellencies on behalf of myself and my men!" And he took a gulp of wine which must have had a temperature of 104 degrees.

But one of the soldiers had remained on foot watchfully prowling round the hut.

Back we got into the carriages. It was now two o'clock— the truly ghastly hour of the Sicilian countryside in summer. We were moving at walking pace, for the slope down towards the Belice river was now starting. All were silent, and the only sound to be heard through the stamp of hooves was the voice of a Carabiniere humming "*La Spag-*

nola sa amar cosi."[1] Dust rose. Then we were across the Belice, a real and proper river for Sicily—it even had water in its bed—and began the interminable ascent at walking pace; bend succeeded bend eternally in the chalky landscape.

It seemed never ending, and yet it did end. At the top of the slope the horses stopped, steaming with sweat; the Carabinieri dismounted, we too alighted to stretch our legs. Then we set off again at a trot.

My mother was now beginning to warn me.

"Watch out now, soon on the left we'll see La Venaría."

In fact we were now passing over a bridge, and there on the left at last glimpsed a little verdure, some bamboo, even a patch or so of orange grove. This was Le Dàgali, the first Cutò property on our road. And behind Le Dàgali was a steep hill, traversed to the top by a wide alley of cypresses leading to La Venaría, a hunting lodge of ours.

We were not far off now. My mother, on tenterhooks because of her love for Santa Margherita, could no longer sit still and kept on craning out of one window or another. "We're nearly at Montevago." "We're home!" Across Montevago we drove, first nucleus of life seen after four hours on the road. What a nucleus though! Wide deserted streets, houses weighed down equally by poverty and by implacable sun, not a living soul, only a few pigs and some cats' carcasses.

---

1   "That's how a Spanish woman loves." (Trs.)

But once past Montevago everything improved. The road was straight and level, the countryside smiling. "There's the Giambalvo villa! There's the Madonna of Graces and its cypresses!" and she even hailed the cemetery with delight. Then the Madonna of Trapani. "We've arrived—there's the bridge!"

It was five in the afternoon. We had been traveling for twelve hours. On the bridge were lined up the municipal band, which broke into a lively polka. Exhausted as we were, with eyebrows white from dust and throats parched, we forced ourselves to smile and thank. A short drive through the streets and we came out into the piazza, saw the graceful tines of our home, and entered its gateway; first courtyard, passageway, second courtyard. We had arrived. At the bottom of the external staircase stood a little group of retainers, headed by our excellent agent Don Nofrio, tiny beneath his white beard and flanked by his powerful wife. "Welcome!" "We're so pleased to have arrived!"

Up in one of the drawing rooms Don Nofrio had prepared crushed ice and lemon drinks, badly made but a blessing all the same. I was dragged off by Anna to my room and plunged, reluctant, into a tepid bath which the agent, peerless man, had thought of having ready, while my wretched parents faced the hordes of acquaintances already beginning to arrive.

IV

The House

SET IN THE MIDDLE of the town, right on the leafy square, it spread over a vast expanse and contained about a hundred rooms, large and small. It gave the impression of an enclosed and self-sufficient entity, of a kind of Vatican as it were, that included staterooms, living rooms, quarters for thirty guests, servants' rooms, three great courtyards, stables and coach houses, a private theater and church a large and very lovely garden, and a big orchard.

And what rooms they were! Prince Niccolò had had the good taste, almost unique for his time, not to ruin the eighteenth-century salons. In the state apartments every door was framed on both sides by fantastic friezes in gray, black or red marble, whose harmonious asymmetry sounded a gay fanfare at everyone passing from one room to another. From the second courtyard a wide balustraded staircase of green marble, in a single flight, led up to a terrace on which opened the great entrance doors, surmounted by the belled cross of the Cutò arms.

These led into a broad entrance hall, its walls entirely covered with two ranks, one above the other, of pictures representing the Filangeri family from 1080 until my grandmother's father; all lifesize standing figures in a great variety of costume, from a Crusader's to a Gentleman's-in-Waiting to Ferdinand II, pictures which in spite of their mediocre workmanship filled the big room with lively familiar presences. Beneath each, in white letters on a black background, were written their names and titles, and the chief events of their lives. "Riccardo, defended Antioch against the Infidels." "Raimondo, wounded in the defence of Acre"; another Riccardo, "chief instigator of the Sicilian Revolt" (that is, of the Sicilian Vespers), Niccolò I "led two Hussar regiments against the Gallic hordes in 1796."

Above each door or window, however, there were the panoramic maps of the "fiefs," then still almost all present and correct. In all four corners were bronze statues of warriors in armor, a concession to the taste of the period, each holding on high a simple oil lamp. On the ceiling Jupiter, wrapped in a lilac cloud, blessed the embarkation of Roger as he prepared to sail from his native Normandy for Sicily; and tritons and water nymphs frolicked around galleys ready to set forth on mother-of-pearl seas.

Once this proud overture was passed though, the house was all grace and charm, or rather gentleness veiled its pride as courtesy does that of an aristocrat. There was a library, its books shut inside cupboards of that decorative eighteenth-century Sicilian style called "Monastic," not unlike the more florid Venetian, but cruder and less sweetened. There was nearly every work of the Enlightenment in tawny leather and gilt binding: *L'Encyclopédie*, Fontenelle, Helvétius, Voltaire in Kehl's great edition (if Maria Carolina read that, what must she have thought?), then *Victoires et Conquêtes*, a collection of Napoleonic bulletins and campaign reports which were my delight in the long silence-filled summer afternoons as I read them sprawled on one of those over-large "poufs" which occupied the center of the ballroom. An odd library, in fact, if one considers that it had been formed by a man as reactionary as that Prince Niccolò. Also to be found there were bound collections of the satirical journals of the Risorgimento, *il Fischietto* and *Lo Spirito Folletto*, some exquisite editions of Don Quixote, of La Fontaine, that rare history of Napoleon with Norvins' charming illustrations (a book I still have); and among moderns the complete works, or almost, of Zola, whose yellow covers showed up glaringly on that mellow background, and a few other lesser novels; but there was also *I Malavoglia*, with an autographed dedication.

I do not know whether I have managed so far to convey the idea that I was a boy who loved solitude, who liked the company of things more than of people. This being the case it will easily be understood how ideal for me was life at Santa Margherita. I would wander through the vast ornate house (twelve people in three hundred rooms) as in an enchanted wood. A wood with no hidden dragons, full of happy marvels, even in the jesting names of the rooms: the "aviary" room, its walls covered in rough crinkled white silk, on which amid infinite festoons of flowering branches glittered tiny multicolored birds painted in by hand; the "*ouistiti*" room where on similar tropical trees swung sly and hairy monkeys; "the rooms of Ferdinando" which evoked at first in me the idea of a fair smiling uncle of mine, but which had actually kept this name because they had been the private apartments of the cruel and jocular *Re Nasone*, as was also shown by the huge Empire "*lit-bateau*," whose mattress was covered in a kind of morocco leather casing, apparently used on royal beds instead of an under blanket; green morocco leather, closely stamped with the triple gilt lilies of Bourbon, and looking like an enormous book. The walls were covered in silk of paler green, with vertical stripes, one shiny and one matte with tiny lines, just like the one in the green drawing room of our house in Palermo. Then in the "tapestry hall," the only one with some sinister association later, hung eight big tapestries on subjects taken from *Gerusalemme Liberata*. In one of these, representing an equestrian joust between Tancredi and Argante, one of the two horses had a strangely human look which I was to link in my mind later with Poe's *House of the Metzengersteins*. This particular tapestry, actually, is still in my possession.

The evenings, oddly enough, we always spent in the

ballroom, an apartment in the center of the first floor with eight balconies looking out over the piazza and four over the first courtyard. It was reminiscent of the ballroom of our house in Palermo; here, too, gold was the dominating note of the room. The walls, on the other hand, were pale green, almost entirely covered with hand-embroidered flowers and golden leaves, and the bases of pillars and the shutters vast as front doors were covered completely in dull gold-leaf with decorations in brighter gold. And when on winter evenings (we actually spent two winters at Santa Margherita, which my mother was loth to leave) we sat in front of the central fireplace, by the glow of a few petrol lamps whose light picked out capriciously a few flowers on the walls and flames in the shutters, we seemed to be enclosed in some magician's cave. I can definitely place the date of one of these evenings because I remember that newspapers were brought in announcing the fall of Port Arthur.

These evenings were not always restricted to the family alone; in fact they seldom were. My mother wanted to keep up her parents' tradition of being on cordial terms with the local notables, and many of these would dine with us in turn, while twice a week everyone met to play *scopone* in the ballroom. My mother had known them since childhood and liked them all; to me they seemed what perhaps they were not, good people without exception. Among them there was a native of Palermo forced by his wretched financial condition to emigrate to Santa

Margherita, where he had a tiny house and an even tinier patch of ground; he was a practiced shot, had been a close friend of my grandfather's, and enjoyed particularly favorable treatment; I think he used to lunch with us every day and was the only one to call my mother "*tu*," which she returned with a respectful "*lei*." He was a straight-backed, wiry old man, with blue eyes and long white sprouting moustaches, distinguished and even elegant in his well-cut if threadbare clothes. I suspect now that he may have been a bastard of the Cutò family, some uncle of my mother's in fact. He would play the piano and tell wonderful tales of shooting out in the wilds and woods with my grandfather, of the prodigious acumen of his gundogs (Diana and Furetta) and of alarming but ever innocuous encounters with the brigand bands of Leone and Capraro. Then there was Nenè Giaccone, a big local landowner, with his flamboyant little goatee and insatiable vivacity; he was highly esteemed in the town as a great *viveur* because he spent two months of every year in Palermo at the Hotel Milano, on Via Emerico Amari, opposite the side façade of the Politeama—this was considered fast.

There was the Cavaliere Mario Rossi, a little man with a small black beard; he was an old post-office clerk who talked of nothing but Frascati ("You must realize, duchess, that Frascati is almost Rome") where his duties had taken him for a few months. There was Ciccio Neve, with his big rubicund face and mutton-chop whiskers à la Franz-Josef, who lived with a mad sister (when one knows a Si-

cilian village well one discovers innumerable lunatics);
there was Catania the schoolmaster, bearded like Mo-
ses; and another landowner, Montalbano, the typical
rustic lordling, obtuse and gross, the father, I believe, of
the present Communist member of Parliament; Giorgio
di Giuseppe, the intellectual of the company, from beneath whose windows passersby at night heard him playing Chopin's nocturnes on the piano; Giambalvo, hugely
fat and full of fun; Doctor Monteleone with a little black
beard, who had studied in Paris and often spoke of the
Rue Monge where he had had the oddest adventures; Don
Colicchio Terrasa, very old and almost wholly peasant,
with his son Totò, a great trencherman; and many others
who were seen more rarely.

It will be noticed these were one and all men. Wives,
daughters, sisters stayed at home, both because women in
the country (in 1905–14) did not pay social calls, and also
because their husbands, fathers and brothers did not con-
sider them presentable. My mother and father would go
and visit them once a season, and with Mario Rossi, whose
wife was a Bilella and famous for her gastronomic arts,
they would even take luncheon now and again; sometimes
after a complex system of signals and warnings, she would
send over by a small boy, who came galloping across the
piazza under the broiling sun, an immense tureen full
of macaroni done with barley in the Sicilian mode with
chopped meat, eggplant and basil, which was, I remember, truly a dish fit for rustic and primitive gods. The boy

had precise orders to set this on the dining table when we were already sitting down and, before leaving, he would say: "*A signura raccumanna: 'u cascavaddu*" ("The signora recommends: cacciocavallo cheese"); an injunction perhaps sage but never obeyed.

The one exception to this absence of women was Margherita, the daughter of Nené Giaccone the *viveur*; a pretty girl with auburn hair like her father, she had been educated at the Sacred Heart and was to be seen every now and then.

In contrast to the cordial relations with the townsfolk, those with the authorities were strained; the Mayor, Don Pietro Giaccone, was not on the visiting list, and neither was the parish priest, for all that the Cutò family had the benefice in their gift. The Mayor's absence is explained by the continuous feuding with the Town Hall over "civic customs." The Mayor was also a ladies' man and for a while he kept a trollop who passed herself off for a Spaniard, Pepita; he had unearthed her in a café-concert at Agrigento (!) and she drove about the streets of the town in a trap drawn by a gray pony. One day, as my father was standing outside the front entrance, he saw the couple passing in their elegant equipage; and with the unerring eye he had for these things he noticed that the wheel hub had come away from its mounting and the wheel was on the point of falling off; so although he was not acquainted with the Mayor and their relations were strained, he ran after the trap shouting: "Cavaliere look out, your right wheel's coming off."

The Mayor stopped, saluted with his whip and said: "Thank you. I'll see to it." And he resumed his way without dismounting. Another twenty yards and the wheel did indeed go off after its own purposes, and the Mayor was rudely thrown to the ground together with Pepita in her pink chiffon dress. They were but slightly hurt. The following day four partridges arrived and a visiting card: "Cav. Pietro Giaccone, Mayor of Santa Margherita Belice, to thank for the good but unheeded advice." But this symptom of a thaw had no sequel.

V

The Garden

IN THE SANTA MARGHERITA house, the last and biggest of the three courtyards was the "courtyard of the palms"; it was planted all over with the tallest of palm trees which in that season were laden with clusters of unfertilized dates. Entering it from the passage leading from the second courtyard, one had on one's right the long and low line of the building that housed the stables with, beyond it, the riding school. In the center of the courtyard, to the left of the stables and riding school, stood two high pillars in porous yellow stone, adorned with masks and scrolls, which opened on to flights of steps leading down into the garden. They were short flights (a dozen or so steps in all) but in that space the baroque architect had found ways of expressing a freakish and whimsical turn of mind, alternating high and low steps, subjecting the flights to the most unexpected distortions, creating superfluous little landings with niches and benches so as to produce in this small space a variety of possible joinings and

separations, of brusque rejections and affectionate recon-
ciliations, which imparted to the staircase the atmosphere
of a lovers' tiff.

The garden, like so many others in Sicily, was designed
on a level lower than the house, I think so that advan-
tage could be taken of a spring welling up there. It was
very large and, when seen from a window of the house,
perfectly regular in its complicated system of alleys and
paths. It was all planted out with ilex and araucaria, the
alleys bordered with myrtle hedges; and in the furnace of
summer, when the jet of the spring dwindled, it was a paradise of parched scents of origanum and calamint, as are
so many gardens in Sicily that seem made to delight the
nose rather than the eyes.

The long alleys surrounding it on all four sides were
the only straight ones in the whole garden, for in the
rest the designer (who must surely have been the whimsical architect of the stairs) had multiplied twists, turns,
mazes and corridors, contributing to give it that tone of
graceful mystery which enveloped the whole house. All
these cross-alleys, however, came out eventually on to a
big central clearing, the one where the spring had been
found; this, now enclosed in an ornate prison, lightened
with its spurts a great fountain in the center of which, on
an islet of artificial ruins, a disheveled and ungirt goddess
of Abundance poured torrents of water into a deep basin
forever crossed by friendly ripples. It was bounded by a
balustrade, surmounted here and there by tritons and ne-

reids sculptured in the act of diving with movements that were disordered in each individual statue but fused into a scenic whole. All round the fountain were stone benches, darkened by centuries-old moss, protected from sun and wind by a tangle of foliage.

But for a child the garden was brimful of surprises. In a corner was a big conservatory filled with cacti and rare shrubs, the kingdom of Nino, head gardener and my great friend, he, too, red-haired like so many at Santa Margherita, perhaps owing to the Norman Filangeri. There was a bamboo thicket, growing thick and sturdy around a secondary fountain, in the shade of which was an open space for games, with a swing from which long before my time Pietro Scalea, later Minister of War, fell and broke his arm. In one of the side alleys, embedded in the wall, was a big cage destined at one time for monkeys, in which my cousin Clementina Trigona and I shut ourselves one day, a Sunday morning when the garden was open to the townsfolk who stopped in mute amazement to gaze, uncertainly, at these dressed-up simians. There was a "dolls' house," built for the diversion of my mother and her four sisters, made of red brick, with window frames in *pietra serena*; now, with its roof and floors fallen in, it was the only disconsolate corner of the big garden, the remainder of which Nino kept in admirable order with every tree well pruned, every alley yellow-pebbled, every bush clipped.

Every two weeks or so a cart came up from the nearby Belice with a big barrel full of eels, which were unloaded into the secondary fountain (the one of the bamboos), that served as a fishpond, when the cook sent for them to be scooped out with little nets according to the needs of the kitchen.

Everywhere at corners of alleys rose figures of obscure gods, usually noseless; and as in every self-respecting Eden there was a serpent hidden in the shadows, in the shape of some castor-oil shrubs (lovely in other ways with their oblong green leaves bordered in red) which one day gave me a nasty surprise when, crushing the berries of a fine vermilion bunch, I recognized upon the air the smell of the oil that, at that happy age, was the only real shadow on my life. My beloved Tom was following me, and I held out my besmirched hand for him to sniff; I still can see the kindly and reproachful way in which he puckered half of his black lip, as well brought-up dogs do when they want to show their disgust without giving offense to their masters.

A garden, I have said, full of surprises. But the whole of Santa Margherita was that, full of cheerful little traps. One would open a door on a passage and glimpse a perspective of rooms dim in the shade of half-pulled shutters, their walls covered with French prints representing Bonaparte's campaigns in Italy; at the top of the stairs leading to the second floor was a door that was almost invisible, so narrow was it and flush with the wall, and behind this was a big room crammed with old pictures hung right up to the very top of the walls, as in prints of the Paris *Salon* in the eighteenth century. One of the ancestral portraits in the first room was hinged, and behind lay my grandfather's gun rooms, for he was a great shot.

The trophies shut in glass cabinets were local only: crimson-footed partridges, disconsolate-looking woodcock, coots from the Belice; but a big bench with scales, little measures for preparing cartridges, glass-fronted cupboards full of multicolored cartridge cases, colored prints showing more dangerous adventures (I can still see a bearded explorer in white fleeing screaming before the charge of a greenish rhinoceros), all these were enchantments to an adolescent. On the walls also hung prints and photographs of gundogs, pointers and setters, showing the calm of all canine faces. The guns were ranged in big racks, ticketed with numbers corresponding to a register in which were recorded the shots fired from each. It was from one of these guns, I think a lady's, with two richly damascened barrels, that I fired, in the garden, the first and last shots of my sporting career; one of the bearded keepers forced me to shoot at some innocent redbreasts; two fell, unfortunately, with blood on their tepid gray plumage; and as they were still quivering the keeper wrung their necks with his fingers.

In spite of my readings of "*Victoires et Conquêtes*," and "*L'épée de l'intrépide général comte Delort rougie du sang des ennemis de l'Empire*" this scene horrified me: apparently I only like blood when metamorphosed into printer's ink. I went straight to my father, to whose orders this slaughter of the Innocents was due, and said that never again would I fire on any creature.

Ten years later I was to kill a Bosnian with a pistol and who knows how many other Christians by shellfire. But this never made on me a tenth of the impression left by those two wretched robins.

There was also the "carriage room," a great, dark chamber, in which stood two enormous eighteenth-century *carrosses*, one gala, all gilt and glass, with doors on whose panels, against a yellow background, were painted pastoral scenes in *"vernis Martin"*; its seats, for at least six persons, were of faded taffeta; the other, a traveling carriage, was olive green with gilt edgings and coats-of-arms on the door panels, and was upholstered in green morocco leather. Beneath the seats there were lined cupboards intended, I think, for provisions on a journey, but now containing only a solitary silver dish.

Then there was the "children's kitchen" with a miniature range and a set of copper cooking implements to scale, which my grandmother had installed in a vain attempt to inveigle her daughters into learning to cook.

And then there was the church and the theater, with the fairy-tale passages by which they were reached, but of those I will speak later.

Amid all these splendors I slept in a completely bare room overlooking the garden, called the "pink room" because of the color of its varnished plaster; on one side was a dressing room with a strange oval brass bath raised on

four high wooden legs. I remember the baths which I was
made to take in water that had starch dissolved in it or
bran in a little bag from which when wet came a scented,
milky drip: *bains de son*, bran baths, traces of which can be
found in memoirs of the Second Empire, a habit which
had evidently been handed on to my mother by my grandmother.

In a room nearby, identical to mine, but blue, slept a
succession of governesses, Anna I and Anna II, who were
German, and Mademoiselle, who was French. At my
bedhead hung a kind of Louis Seize showcase in white
wood, enclosing three ivory statuettes of the Holy Family on a crimson background. This case has been miraculously salvaged and now hangs at the bedhead of the
room in which I sleep at my cousin Piccolo's villa at Capo
d'Orlando. In that villa, too, I retrieve not only the "Holy
Family" of my infancy, but a trace, faint certainly but un-
mistakable, of my childhood; and so I love going there.

VI

The Church and the Theater

THERE WAS ALSO the church, which was then the cathedral of Santa Margherita. From the carriage room one turned left and, up a few steps, reached a wide passage ending in a kind of schoolroom with benches, blackboards, and relief maps, where my mother and aunts had done their lessons as children.

It was at Santa Margherita, at the not-so-tender age of eight, that I was taught to read. To begin with, others read aloud to me; on alternate days, that is Tuesdays, Thursdays and Saturdays, "Sacred History" and a kind of potted version of the Bible and the Gospels; and on Mondays, Wednesdays and Fridays, classical mythology. So I acquired a "solid" knowledge of both these disciplines; I am still capable of saying how many, and who, were the brothers of Joseph and of finding my way among the complicated family squabbles of the Atrides. Before I learnt to read for myself my grandmother was forced by her own goodness to read aloud for an hour from *The Queen of the*

Caribbean by Salgari; and I can still see her trying hard not to fall asleep as she read out about the prowess of the Black Pirate and the swashbuckling of Carmaux.

Eventually it was decided that this religious, classic, and adventuresome culture, vicariously imparted, could not last much longer, and that I was to be handed over to Donna Carmela, an elementary schoolmistress at Santa Margherita. Nowadays elementary schoolmistresses are smart lively young ladies, who chatter about Pestalozzi's and James's pedagogic studies and want to be called "*Professoressa.*" In 1905, in Sicily, an elementary schoolmistress was an old woman more than half-peasant, with her spectacled head wrapped up in a black shawl; but actually this one was a most expert teacher, and within two months I knew how to read and write and had lost my doubts about double consonants and accented syllables. For whole weeks, in the "blue room" separated from my pink room only by the passage, I had to carry out articulated dictations—ar-ti-cu-la-ted dic-ta-tions—and repeat dozens of times, "di, do, da, fo, fa, fu, *qui* and *qua* don't take an accent." Blessed labors! Thanks to them it will never be my lot, as it has been the lot of a distinguished senator, to be surprised at the frequency with which newspapers and handbills incur the error of slipping an extra *b* into "Republic."

When I had learnt to write Italian my mother taught me to write French; I already spoke it and had often been to Paris and in France, but it was now that I learnt to read French. I can still see my mother sitting with me at a desk, writing slowly and very clearly *le chien, le chat, le cheval* in the columns of an exercise book with a shiny blue cover, and teaching me that what the French pronounce as "ch" the Italians pronounce as "sh," "like 'scirocco and Sciacca,'" she would say. From then on, until my school days, I spent all my afternoons in my grandparents' apartments at Via di Lampedusa, reading behind a screen. At five o'clock my grandfather would call me into his study to give me my afternoon refreshment a hunk of hard bread and a large glass of cold water. This has remained my favorite drink ever since.

Before reaching the schoolroom there were two doors on the left which led to three guest rooms; these were most favored because they gave on to the terrace on which the entrance stairway abutted. On the right of the carriage room, between two white console tables, was a big yellow door. From this one entered a small oblong room, its chairs and various tables loaded with images of Saints; I can still see a big china dish in the middle of which lay the head of St John the Baptist, life-size, with blood coagulated in the bottom. From this room one entered a gallery at the level of a high first story, looking straight on to the High Altar, which was surrounded by a superb railing of flowery gilt. In this gallery were prie-dieux, chairs, and innumerable rosaries, and from it every Sunday at eleven we attended High Mass, sung without excessive fervor. The church itself was a fine spacious one, I remember, in Empire style, with large, ugly frescoes in white stucco work on the ceiling, as in the Olivella church in Palermo which it resembled, albeit on a smaller scale.

From this same carriage room which, I now remember, was a kind of revolving stage for the least frequented part of the house, one penetrated to the right into a series of passages, cubbyholes and staircases that gave one a sense of having no outlet, like certain dreams and eventually reached the corridor of the theater. This was a real and proper theater, with two tiers each of twelve boxes, as well as a main box and, of course, the stalls. The auditorium, capable of holding at least three hundred people, was all white and gold, with its seats and the walls of boxes lined in very light blue velvet. The style was Louis Seize, restrained and elegant. In the center was the equivalent of the royal box, that is, our box, surmounted by an enormous shield of gilt wood, containing the belled cross set on a double-headed eagle's breast. And the drop curtain, rather later in date, represented the defense of Antioch by Riccardo Filangeri (a defense which, according to Grousset, was far less heroic than the painter gave one to believe).

The auditorium was lit by gilt petrol lamps set on brackets projecting under the first tier of boxes.

The best of it was that this theater (which of course also had a public entrance from the piazza) was often used.

Every now and again a company of actors would arrive; these were strolling players who, generally in summer, moved on carts from one village to the other, staying two or three days in each to give performances. In Santa Margherita where there was a proper theater they stayed longer, two or three weeks.

At ten in the morning the leading actor would call in frock coat and top hat to ask for permission to perform in the theater; he would be received by my father or, in his absence, by my mother, who of course gave permission, refused any rent (or rather made a contract for a token rental of fifty *centesimi* for the two weeks), and also paid a subscription for our own box. After which the leading actor left, to return half-an-hour later and request a loan of furniture. These companies traveled, in fact, with a few bits of painted scenery but no stage furniture, which would have been too costly and inconvenient to carry about. The furniture was granted, and in the evening we would recognize our armchairs, tables and wardrobes on the stage (they were not our best, I'm sorry to say). They were handed back punctually at the moment of departure, sometimes so garishly revarnished that we had to ask other companies to desist from this well-intentioned practice. Once, if I remember right, the leading lady also called on us, a fat good-natured Ferrarese of about thirty who was to play *La Dame aux Camélias* for the closing night. Finding her own wardrobe unsuitable for the solemnity of the occasion she came to ask my mother for an evening dress: and so the

Lady of the Camellias appeared in a very low-cut robe of Nile green covered in silver spangles.

These companies wandering round country villages have now vanished, which is a pity. The scenery was primitive, the acting obviously bad; but they played with gusto and fire and their "presence" was certainly more lifelike than are the pallid shades of fifth-rate films now shown in the same villages.

Every night there was a play, and the repertoire was most extensive; the whole of nineteenth-century drama passed on that stage; Scribe, Rovetta, Sardou, Giacometti and Torelli. Once there was even a *Hamlet*, the first time in fact that I ever heard it. And the audience, partly of peasants, were attentive and warm in their applause. At Santa Margherita, at least, these companies did good business, with theater and furniture free and their draught horses put up and foddered in our stables.

I used to attend every night, except on one night of the season called "black night," when some French *pochade*, reputed indecent, was shown. Next day our local friends came to report on this libertine performance, and were usually very disappointed as they had expected something much more salacious.

I enjoyed it all enormously, and so did my parents. The better companies at the end of their season were offered a kind of rustic garden party with a simple but abundant buffet out in the garden, which cheered up the stomachs, often empty I fear, of those excellent strolling players.

But already in the last year in which I spent a long period at Santa Margherita, 1921, companies of actors no longer came, and instead flickering films were shown. The war had killed off, among others, these poor and picturesque wandering companies which had their own artistic merits and were, I have an idea, the training school of many a great Italian actor and actress of the nineteenth century, Duse among others.

VII

Excursions

OF ALL THE WALKS around Santa Margherita, that towards Montevago was our most frequent, for it ran level,
was the right length (about two miles each way), and had
a definite if not attractive goal; Montevago itself.

Then there was a walk in the opposite direction, on the
main road towards Misilbesi; one passed under a huge
umbrella pine and then over the Dragonara bridge, surrounded unexpectedly by thick, wild verdure which re-
minded me of scenes from Ariosto as I imagined them
at that period from Doré's illustrations. The landscape
around Misilbesi had a ruffianly air about it suggestive
of violence and hardship of a sort I imagined was no longer to be found in Sicily; a few years ago I noticed a by-
road near Santa Ninfa (called Rampinzeri) in which I recognized the same ruffianly yet amiable aspect I associated
with Misilbesi. On reaching Misilbesi, a sunbaked cross-
roads marked by an old house with three dusty and de-

serted tracks that seemed to be leading to Hades rather than to Sciacca or Sambuca, we generally returned by carriage as our usual four miles were by then greatly exceeded.

The carriage had followed us at walking pace, stopping every now and again so as not to overtake us and then rejoining us unhurriedly; phases of silence and of disappearance alternating according to the turns of the road, before we were caught up with a clatter.

In autumn our walks had as goal the vineyard of Toto Ferrara, where we would sit on stones and eat the sweetest mottled grapes (vine grapes, for in 1905 table grapes were scarcely ever cultivated in our region), after which we entered a room in semidarkness; at the end of it a lusty young man was jerking like a madman inside a barrel, his feet squashing the grapes whose greenish juice could be seen flowing down a wooden channel, while the air was filled with a heavy smell of must.

"Dance, and Provençal song, and sunburnt mirth."[1]

No, no "mirth" at all; in Sicily there was none, there never is even now during work: the Tuscan girls singing their *stornelli* at vintage, the threshing punctuated by feasting, song and lovemaking round Leghorn, these are things unknown; all work is *'na camurrìa*,[2] a blasphemous contravention of the eternal repose granted by the gods to our "lotus-eaters."

1 Keats: "Ode to a Nightingale."
2 In Sicilian, venereal disease and, by extension, vexation, affliction.

On rainy afternoons of autumn our walk was confined to the public gardens. These were set at the northern limit of the town, on a hillside overlooking the great valley which is probably the main east-west axis of Sicily and is certainly one of its few outstanding geographical features.

These gardens had been given to the municipality by my grandfather and were of quite infinite melancholy; a longish alley bordered by young cypresses and old ilexes led to a bare open space facing a small shrine of the Madonna of Trapani, with a flowerbed of parched yellow bamboos in the middle and on the left a kind of kiosk-temple with a round dome from which to gaze at the view.

And it was worth gazing at. Opposite stretched a vast range of low mountains, all yellow from reaping, with blackish patches of burnt stubble, so that one had a vivid impression of a monstrous crouching beast. On the flanks of this lioness or hyena (according to the eye of the beholder) could just be made out villages whose grayish-yellow stone was scarcely distinguishable from the background: Poggioreale, Contessa, Salaparuta, Gibellina, Santa Ninfa, all weltering in poverty and dog days, and in an ignorance against which they never reacted with even the faintest of flickers.

The little shrine at the other side of the open space in the gardens was a target for anticlerical manifestos by Santa Margherita's law students, there on vacation. Often could be seen written up in pencil strophes from Carducci's

"Hymn to Satan": "*Salute, o Satana, o ribellione, o forza vindice della ragione.*"[1] And when my mother (who knew the "Hymn to Satan" by heart and whose lack of admiration for it was due to aesthetic reasons alone) next morning sent Nino our gardener to put a coat of whitewash over the modestly sacrilegious verses, others appeared two days later: "*Ti scomunico, o prete, vate di lutti e d'ire*"[2] and other volleys which the good Giosuè[3] thought it his duty to discharge against citizen Mastai.[4]

On the slope below the kiosk could be gathered capers, which I did regularly at the risk of breaking my neck; and around there also, it seems, were to be found those Spanish flies whose pulverized heads make such a potent aphrodisiac. I was sure at the time that these flies were there; but whom I heard this from, or when or how, remains a mystery. Never in my life, at any rate, have I set eyes on Spanish flies, dead or alive, whole or in powder.

Such were our daily, not very exacting, walks. Then there were longer, more complicated ones, our excursions.

The chief excursion of all was that to La Venaría, a hunting lodge on a spur just before Montevago. This was an excursion always made with local guests twice or so in a season, and was never without an element of comedy. A decision would be reached: "Next Sunday, lunch at Ve-

---

1   "Greetings, oh Satan, oh rebellion, oh avenging force of reason."
2   "I excommunicate you, oh priest, prophet mourning and wrath."
3   Carducci.
4   Pope Pius IX.

naría." And in the morning off we would set at ten o'clock, ladies in carriages, men on donkeys. Although all or almost all the men owned horses or at least mules, the use of donkeys was traditional; the only rebel was my father, who got round the difficulty by declaring himself to be the one person capable of driving, on those roads, the dogcart conveying the ladies and bearing also, in the dog-cages secreted under the box, bottles and cakes for the guests' luncheon.

Amid laughter and jest the company would take the road to Montevago. In the middle of the dusty group was the dogcart in which my mother, with Anna or whichever Mademoiselle was with us, Margherita Giaccone and some other lady, tried to shelter from the dust with gray veils of almost Moslem thickness; around would prance the donkeys (or rather " 'i scecche," for in Sicilian donkeys are almost always feminine, like ships in English) their ears flapping. There were real falls, genuine donkeys' mutinies, and pretended falls due to love of the picturesque. We crossed Montevago, arousing vocal protests from every dog in the place, reached the Dàgari bridge, dropped down into the adjacent depression and began climbing.

The avenue was really grandiose; about three hundred yards long, it went straight up towards the top of the hill, bordered on each side by a double row of cypresses; not adolescent cypresses like those of San Guido, but great trees[1]

---

1   Now felled by later owners.

almost a hundred years old, whose thick branches spread their austere scent in every season. The rows of trees were interrupted every now and again by sets of benches, and once by a fountain with a great mask emitting water at intervals. Under the odorous shade we climbed towards La Venaría, bathed in full sunshine high above.

It was a hunting lodge built at the end of the eighteenth century, considered "tiny," though actually it must have had at least twenty rooms. Built on top of the hill, on the opposite side to the one by which we approached, it looked sheer across the valley, the same valley to be seen from the public gardens, which from higher up seemed vast and even desolate.

Cooks had left that morning at seven and had already prepared everything; when a boy lookout announced the group's approach they thrust into the ovens their famous *timbales* of macaroni *alla Talleyrand*, (the only macaroni which keeps for a period), so that when we arrived we had scarcely time to wash our hands before going straight out on to the terrace, where two tables had been laid in the open air. In the *timbales* the macaroni were steeped in the lightest glaze and, beneath the savory crust of flaky pastry, absorbed the flavor of the prosciutto and truffles sliced into match-like slivers.

Huge cold bass with mayonnaise followed, then stuffed turkey and avalanches of potatoes. One might expect strokes from overeating. A fat guest, Giambalvo, nearly did pass out once: but a pailful of cold water in his face

and a prudent nap in a shady room saved him. Next, all
was put to rights by the arrival of one of those iced cakes
at which Marsala, the cook, was a past master. Wines, as
always in sober Sicily, were of no importance. The guests
expected them, of course, and liked their glasses filled to
the brim ("no collars" they would call to the footman), but
in the absence of a collar to their glasses they emptied but
one, at the most two.

After dusk we descended homeward.

I have spoken of excursions in the plural; in fact our only
real excursion, thinking it over, was that to La Venaría.
In the first years there were others, of which however I
have kept only rather vague memories; though the word
"vague" is not quite exact; a better phrase would be "dif-
ficult to describe." The visual impression has remained
vivid in my mind but was not then linked to any word. We
must have taken the carriage out to Sciacca, for instance,
to lunch with the Bertolinos when I was five or six years
old; but of the luncheon, the people we met, the journey,
I have no memory at all. On the other hand of Sciacca itself, or rather of its promenade above the sea, such a pho-
tographic, complete, and precise image has remained
stamped on my mind that when I returned there a couple
of years ago, for the first time after more than fifty years, I
was easily able to compare the scene under my eyes with
the old one that had remained in my mind, and note the
many similarities and the few differences.

As always memories refer particularly to memories of "light"; at Sciacca I see a very blue, almost black, sea glinting furiously beneath the midday sun, in one of those skies of high Sicilian summer which are misty with heat, a balustrade over a sheer drop to the sea, a kind of kiosk, to the left of which was a café—which is still there.

Looming skies with scudding rain clouds, on the other hand, remind me of a small country house, Cannitello, near Catania, set on a steep hillside reached by a zigzagging road which, I don't know why, horses had to ascend at a gallop. I see a landau with dusty blue cushions (the very fact they were blue showed that the carriage was not our own but hired), my mother sitting in a corner, panic-stricken herself but trying to reassure me, while beside us the stunted trees whirled past and vanished with the speed of wind, and the coachman's incitements mingled with whip cracks and frenzied tingling of collar bells (no, that carriage was certainly not ours).

Of the house where we were going I retain a memory of what I can now say was its gentlemanly but poverty-stricken air; obviously I did not formulate this economic-social judgment at the time, but I can say it in all serenity now, examining the mental photograph recently retrieved from the archives of memory.

I have spoken of the people who belonged to the household at Santa Margherita; I have yet to mention the guests who came to stay for a period of days or weeks.

I have to say that these guests were few; there were

no motorcars then, or rather three or four at most in the whole of Sicily, and the ghastly state of the roads induced the owners of the *rarae aves* to use them only in towns. Santa Margherita was a long way from Palermo, then, a twelve-hour journey—and what a journey!

Amongst the guests at Santa Margherita I remember my Aunt Giulia Trigona with her daughter Clementina and the girl's nanny, a bony German woman, extremely strict and quite unlike my smiling Annas. Giovanna (now Albanese) was not yet born, and as for Uncle Romualdo, I don't know where he displayed his splendid physique and his impeccable attire.

Clementina was, and still is, a male in skirts. Blunt, resolute, truculent as she was (the very qualities which were later to turn out to her detriment), she proved a quite acceptable playmate for a little boy of six or seven. I well recall those endless pursuits, mounted on tricycles, which took place not only in the garden but indoors as well, between the entrance hall and the "Leopold drawing room"; there and back they must have added up to a good four hundred yards.

I've already mentioned the business of our transformation into monkeys in the garden cage; and I remember the breakfasts eaten round an iron table in the garden. I fear, though, that this latter may be a "pseudo-recollection": a photograph exists of these breakfasts in the garden, and it could very well be that I am confusing the actual recollection of the photograph with an archaic memory of childhood. This is by no means impossible, and indeed it happens all the time.

I have to say I possess no recollection of my Aunt Giulia, on this occasion; probably Clementina and I were still of an age to take our meals separately.

On the other hand I have the most vivid memory of Giovannino Cannitello. He was the proprietor of the Cannitello mansion already mentioned. Giovanni Gerbino-Xaxa, baron of Cannitello, was his full name, and he belonged to a good local family, feudatories of the Filangeri; for the Filangeri had the right, very rare and much envied, of investing with a barony a total of two of their own vassals in every generation. The Gerbinos (who had been judges of the High Court way back under the Empire) had been granted this privilege, and my grandmother even used to call him "the very first vassal among my vassals."

Giovannino Cannitello then gave me the impression of being an old man; actually he could not have been more than forty. He was very tall, very thin, very shortsighted; in spite of his spectacles, which were a *pince-nez* and had extraordinarily thick lenses, squashing down his nose with their weight, he used to walk bent in the hope of recognizing at least a vague shadow of his surroundings.

A good, sensitive person, well liked and of no great intelligence, he had dedicated his life (and spent the greater part of his fortune) to trying to be "a man of fashion." And from the point of view of dress he had certainly succeeded; never have I seen a man with a wardrobe more sober, better cut, or less showy than his. He had been one of the moths drawn by the glamorous glow of the Florios, and who, after many a dizzy pirouette, dropped on to the tablecloth with burnt wings. He had been more than once to Paris with the Florios and even put up at the Ritz; and of Paris (the Paris of *boîtes*, of luxurious brothels, of high-priced ladies) he had preserved a dazzled memory which made him remarkably like the Doctor Monteleone I have mentioned before; with the difference that the engineer's memories were based on the Latin quarter and the Ecole de Médecine. They were not on very good terms, Giovannino Cannitelio and Doctor Monteleone, perhaps because of their rivalry in disputing the favors of the Ville Lumière. There was a long-standing family joke about Doctor Monteleone being woken in the night because Cannitello had swallowed a liter of paraffin with a view to suicide (having been jilted by a pretty chambermaid); and he had simply turned over on his other side saying: "Shove a wick in his stomach and set it alight."

This because Giovannino Cannitello (who subsequent to the French period with Mademoiselle Sempell acquired the nickname "le grand Esco," that is, Spindleshanks) was temperamentally inclined to a vigorous pursuit of the ladies. And there is no counting the times that he made attempts on his life (by means of a circumspect use of paraffin, or brazier fumes by open window) after suffering rejection at the hands of his beloved, who generally belonged below stairs.

Poor Cannitello became almost blind and utterly destitute before he died not so many years ago (about 1932) in his house on Via Alloro, next door to the Coachmen's church. My mother, who went to visit him until the end, would return much affected by his being so bent that, when sitting in his armchair, his face was eight inches from the floor, and to talk to him she had to sit on a cushion on the very floor itself.

In the early years Alessio Cerda was also a frequent guest at Santa Margherita. Then he went blind, and although we always saw him at Palermo, he made no further appearances at Santa Margherita. There was a photograph of him dressed in his uniform as lieutenant in the *Guide*, with the soft cap, soft boots, soft gloves of our unfortunate army of 1866; all this softness was to find itself asserted at Custozza.[1] But of Alessio Cerda, a most singular personality, I shall have occasion to speak.

Another person who came once, and came indeed in one of the first motorcars, was Paolo Scaletta. I think he arrived on an off-chance: he was on his way to some Valdina properties at Menfi, not far from Santa Margherita, when his car broke down. And he came to seek our hospitality.

Many of my memories center on Santa Margherita—agreeable and disagreeable, but all of them crucial.

---

1   A village near Verona where in June 1866 the Austrians under the archduke Albert routed an Italian army led by King Victor Emmanuel.

VIII

The Pink Dining Room

But I realize that I have forgotten to mention the dining
room, which was singular for various reasons; singular for existing at all; in an eighteenth-century house it
was very rare, I think, to have a room set apart as a dining room: at that time people dined in any drawing room,
changing continually, as in fact I still do now.

But there was one at Santa Margherita. Not very big,
it could only hold about twenty chairs comfortably. It
looked out over two balconies on to the second courtyard.
Three doors gave access to it: the principal door, which led
into the "picture gallery" (not the one I have already mentioned), a second which led into the "huntsmen's room,"
and the third giving on to the "office," whence the rope-
pulley lift communicated with the kitchen below. These
doors were white, Louis Seize, and had big panels with
decorations in relief, gilt, of a greenish dull gold. From the
ceiling hung a Murano chandelier, whose grayish glass
showed up the color of floral designs.

Prince Alessandro, who arranged this room, had thought up the idea of asking a local artist to paint on the walls pictures of himself and his family while actually eating their meals. These were large pictures on canvas, completely covering a wall from floor to ceiling with virtually life-size figures.

One showed breakfast: the prince and princess, he in green shooting clothes, boots and wearing a hat, she in white *déshabillé* but wearing jewels, sitting at a small table intent on taking chocolate, served by a little negro slave in a turban. She was holding out a biscuit to an impatient hound, he raising towards his mouth a big blue cup decorated with flowers. Another picture represented a picnic: a number of ladies and gentlemen were sitting around a tablecloth spread in a field and covered with splendid-looking pasties and grass-plaited bottles; in the background could be seen a fountain, and the trees were young and low. This, I think, must have been the actual garden of Santa Margherita just after it was planted.

A third picture, the biggest, represented a formal dinner party with the gentlemen in very curly wigs and the ladies in full evening dress. The princess was wearing a delicious robe of silver pink *broché* silk, with a dog collar round her neck and a great *parure* of rubies on her bosom. Footmen in full livery and cordons were entering bearing high dishes elaborately decorated.

There were another two pictures, but I can only remember the subject of one of them, for it was always facing me; this was the children's afternoon refreshment. Two little girls of ten and twelve years of age, powdered and tightly laced into their pointed bodices, sat facing a boy of about fifteen, dressed in an orange-colored suit with black facings and carrying a rapier, and an old lady in black (certainly the governess): all were eating large ices of an odd pink color, maybe of cinnamon, rising in sharp cones from long glass goblets.

Another of the oddities of the house was the table-center in the dining room. This was a large fixed silver ornament, surmounted by Neptune who threatened the guests with his trident, while beside him an Amphitrite eyed them with a hint of malice. The whole was set on a rock rising in the middle of a silver basin, surrounded by dolphins and marine monsters squirting water from their mouths through some machinery hidden in a central part of the table. It was all very gay and grand, but had the inconvenience of requiring tablecloths with a large hole cut out of the middle for Neptune. (The holes were hidden by flowers or leaves.) There were no sideboards, but four big console tables covered with pink marble, and the general tone of the room was pink, in the marble, in the princess's pink dress, in the big picture, and also in the chair coverings which were pink too, not old but of delicate hue.

For a small boy at Santa Margherita, though, adventure did not lie concealed only in unexplored apartments or in the labyrinth of the garden, but also in so many singular objects. Just think what a source of wonder that table centerpiece could be! But there was also the music box discovered in a drawer: a big clockwork contrivance containing a cylinder set with knobs at irregular intervals, which turned on its own axis and lifted minute steel keys, producing delicate, meticulous melodies.

Near the dining room, in another apartment, were enormous cupboards of yellow wood, the keys of which had been lost; not even Don Nofrio the administrator knew where they were, and when one said that there was no more to be said. After long hesitation the blacksmith was eventually called and the doors were opened. The cupboards contained bed linen, dozens and dozens of sheets, pillowcases, enough for an entire hotel (there were already overwhelming quantities of these in the known cupboards); others contained blankets of real wool scattered with pepper and camphor, still others table linen, small, large or outsize damask tablecloths, all with that hole in the middle. And between one layer and another of this homely treasure were placed little tulle sacks of lavender flowers now in dust. But the most interesting cupboard was one containing writing materials of the eighteenth century; it was a little smaller than the others, and heaped with great sheets of pure rag letter paper, bundles of quill pens tied neatly in dozens, red and blue sealing wafers and very long sticks of sealing wax.

As can be seen, the house of Santa Margherita was a kind of eighteenth-century Pompeii, all miraculously preserved intact: a rare thing always, but almost unique in Sicily which from poverty and neglect is the most destructive of countries. I do not know what were the exact causes of this phenomenal durability: perhaps the fact that my maternal grandfather spent long years there between 1820 and 1840 in a kind of exile imposed on him by the Bourbon kings as a result of a misdemeanor on the Marine Parade at Palermo,[1] or perhaps the passionate care which my grandmother took of it: certainly the fact of her finding in Onofrio Rotolo a unique administrator, the only one who, to my knowledge, was not a thief.

He was still alive in my time: a kind of dwarf with a long white beard, living together with an incredibly large fat wife in one of the many apartments attached to the house, with a separate entrance.

Marvels were recounted of his care and scrupulosity; how, when the house was empty, he went through it every night with lantern in hand to check that all the windows were shut and doors bolted; how he allowed only his wife to wash the precious china; how after a reception (in my grandmother's time) he checked the screws under every chair: how during the winter he spent entire days surveying squads of cleaners polishing and ordering every single object, however out-of-the-way, in that vast house. In spite of his age and anything but youthful aspect his wife was very jealous of him; and ever and again news would reach us of terrific scenes which she made due to her suspicion

---

1 Driving his carriage stark naked.

of his paying too much attention to the charms of some young maidservant. I know for certain that a number of times he protested most vigorously to my mother about her overspending; he was met, needless to say, with a deaf ear and perhaps some contumely.

His death coincided with the rapid and sudden end of this loveliest of lovely country homes. May these lines which no one will read be a homage to its unblemished memory.

Lampedusa

"Lampedusa, for all his self-enclosure, was a writer-in-waiting: he saw more than he was seen." —*The Guardian*

"Every once in a while, like certain golden moments of happiness, infinitely memorable, one stumbles on a book or a writer, and the impact is like an indelible mark."
—*The Independent*

Giuseppe Tomasi di Lampedusa was born in Palermo in 1896. His father was Prince of the island of Lampedusa and Duke of Palma di Montechiaro. The family owned estates around Sicily and enjoyed a posh life up until the First World War. Lampedusa fought and was captured by the Austro-Hungarian army, but managed to escape. After the war he married Alexandra ("Licy") von Stomersee and inherited his father's estate along with his title, Prince of Lampedusa. The family estate was destroyed in the Second World War, and Lampedusa relocated with Licy to Palermo. Lampedusa was always a voracious reader, and toward the end of his life he began the novel that would eventually become *The Leopard*. Rejected by both publishers to whom Lampedusa submitted it, *The Leopard* was published only after his death. It became an international bestseller and was adapted into an award-winning film starring Burt Lancaster.